⊰The New Adventures of⊱

MARY-KATE & ASHLEY ™

The Case Of The

TATTOOED CAT

Look for more great books in

~ The New Adventures of ~
MARY-KATE & ASHLEY™

The Case Of The
TATTOOED CAT

by Heather Alexander

HarperEntertainment
An Imprint of HarperCollins*Publishers*

A PARACHUTE PRESS BOOK

PARACHUTE PRESS

Parachute Publishing, L.L.C.
156 Fifth Avenue
New York, NY 10010

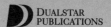
DUALSTAR PUBLICATIONS

Dualstar Publications
c/o Thorne and Company
A Professional Law Corporation
1801 Century Park East
Los Angeles, CA 90067

HarperEntertainment

An Imprint of HarperCollins*Publishers*
10 East 53rd Street, New York, NY 10022

10 9 8 7 6 5 4 3 2 1

1

A SPECIAL CAT

"*Costume*," our teacher, Mrs. Shaw, said. "Zachary Jones, please spell the word *costume*."

That word is easy! I thought. Our class was having a practice spelling bee. It was my turn next.

Zach scratched his wavy brown hair. He took a deep breath, then spelled: "C-o-s-t-o-o-m."

Mrs. Shaw shook her head. "I'm afraid

that is wrong." She pushed her black-rimmed glasses higher onto her pointy nose. "Zach, please sit down."

Zach took a seat with the other kids who were already out of the bee. I smiled at my twin sister, Ashley, who sat in the second row. She is a good speller, but she got a really tricky word wrong.

"Your turn, Mary-Kate," Mrs. Shaw said. "Spell *costume*."

"C-o-s-t-u-m-e," I spelled quickly.

Ashley gave me a thumbs-up.

I made it through three more rounds. The words got harder and harder. Soon my friend Samantha Samuels and I were the only ones left.

"*Autumn*," Mrs. Shaw said. She smiled at me. "Mary-Kate, your word is *autumn*."

I pressed my back up against the chalkboard. The chalk dust tickled my nose. I knew it was important not to rush.

"A-u-t-u-m…" I hesitated. I wasn't sure about the end. Was there a letter after *m*? I tried to sound out the word. "That's it," I finally said.

"Sorry," Mrs. Shaw said. "That was not right." She looked at Samantha. "Your turn now."

Samantha smiled. Her brown eyes sparkled. Even before she opened her mouth, I was sure Samantha knew how to spell the word.

"A-u-t-u-m-n," Samantha said.

"Samantha is the winner!" Mrs. Shaw said. She looked at me. "Good try, Mary-Kate."

Today's spelling bee was just for practice. In a little over a week, on the day after Halloween, we all get to compete in the big spelling bee for the whole school.

Last year Samantha won. This year I wanted to be the school spelling bee

champ. And I knew just how I was going to win....

"I'm going to find the tattooed cat this year," I said on Sunday afternoon.

"Oh, come on, Mary-Kate." Ashley gave my shoulder a little push. "You don't believe the tattooed cat is real, do you?"

"Yes, I do," I said. "And if I find it—I mean, *when* I find it—I'll win the school spelling bee for sure."

Ashley laughed. "You'll win the spelling bee because you've been studying like crazy! Not because of a cat."

Zach and our friend Tim Park stood ahead of us in line at the counter in Chessa's Candies, our favorite candy store. They were buying baseball card packs. Zach owns the most baseball cards in our class.

Zach opened a new pack. He flipped

through the cards. "Look what I got!" he cried. He waved a card in the air.

"What is it?" I asked. It looked like an ordinary baseball card to me.

"This card is totally rare," Zach said. "I've been looking for it for months." He showed it to us. "It's a gold hologram card. When you move the card back and forth, the hologram changes color!"

"Cool!" Tim said. "Want to trade? I'll give you five cards for it."

"No way!" Zach said. He tucked the card in his jacket pocket.

"I heard you guys talking about the tattooed cat," Tim said. "Are you going to look for it this year?"

Ashley whirled around. "You know about the tattooed cat too?"

"Sure," said Tim. "Lots of kids do."

The bell on the candy store door rang. Jane Sommers came in. She's in our class.

She hurried over to us. "What are you guys talking about?" she asked.

"A lucky cat," I said. I paid for a bag of candy corn. Then we all walked to a corner of the store.

"What do you mean, a lucky cat?" Jane asked. She looked surprised.

"Lots of people say that if you see the lucky cat on Halloween and pet it three times before the clock strikes midnight, you can make a wish. And your wish will come true!" I said.

"Wow!" Jane said. "What does the cat look like?"

"It's black," Tim said, "and it's got a white tattoo on its neck in the shape of a jack-o'-lantern."

Jane's eyebrows shot up. "Are you sure? A lucky cat? And it has a real tattoo?"

"Yes," I said. "That's what's supposed to make it lucky."

Ashley shook her head. "There is no such thing as a lucky cat."

"There is so!" Tim said. "I can prove it."

"Really?" I said. This time *my* eyebrows shot up. "Have you seen the cat?"

"No, but…" Tim glanced around. There were lots of kids from school in the candy store.

He lowered his voice. We gathered around him.

"I heard that a kid who goes to Washington Elementary School found the cat last year," Tim said. "My cousin Billy told me."

"That's not proof," Ashley said.

"Ashley is right," I said. "But that doesn't mean the cat isn't real!"

"I still think it is just a story." Ashley looked at her pink plastic watch. "Come on, Mary-Kate. We have to get home."

Ashley and I headed outside. Our friends

came too. We waved good-bye to them and walked down the sidewalk.

"If we see the tattooed cat when we go trick-or-treating, what will you wish for?" I asked.

Ashley shrugged. "I haven't thought about it," she said, "because there is no such thing."

Ashley is always so logical. Sometimes it's fun not to be so logical.

We walked to the corner. That's when I saw it.

I grabbed Ashley's arm. "Look! Do you see what I see?"

Taped to a telephone pole, right in front of us, was a handmade sign. I read the sign out loud: "'Missing cat.'"

I stared at the picture. It was a picture of a black cat. A black cat with a white jack-o'-lantern tattoo!

"It's the tattooed cat!" I yelled.

ONE MORE DETECTIVE

"**W**hat's going on?" Tim asked. He came running down the sidewalk with Jane and Zach.

"The tattooed cat is real!" I jumped up and down.

"I can't believe it," Ashley said. She stared at the picture of the cat. She read the sign out loud: "'Missing cat. My cat, Lucy, is lost. She is black with a white marking on her neck. Reward offered.

Please call 555-5272 for more information.'"

Tim turned to me and Ashley. "This is a case for the Trenchcoat Twins."

Ashley and I are detectives. People call us the Trenchcoat Twins. We run the Olsen and Olsen Detective Agency out of the attic of our house.

"We're taking the case," Ashley said. She pulled her detective notebook and a pencil from her backpack. She copied down the telephone number. "I want to find the tattooed cat. Then I'll prove to all of you that there's no such thing as a lucky cat."

"What do you think the reward is?" Zach asked.

"I don't want to find the cat for the reward," I said. "I have a wish I want to come true. I really want to win the spelling bee!"

"Me too!" Jane said. "Do you think you can find the tattooed cat?"

"We're going to try!" I said.

"The Trenchcoat Twins can find a missing cat—easy!" Tim said.

"Wow! This is a real mystery!" Jane said. "Please, oh, please, can I help?"

"Well…" I hesitated.

"I wouldn't get in the way," Jane promised. "I really want to see how you solve your cases. Please?"

Ashley looked at me and shrugged her shoulders. We never had anyone help us on a case before—except for our dog, Clue. She's our silent partner in the detective agency. She helps us solve cases by sniffing out clues with her nose.

"Okay," I told Jane. "No one hired us to take this case, so you can help."

"Yes!" Jane said. Her face shone with excitement. "What do we do first?"

"First we have to make a phone call. Come on!" Ashley said.

The three of us ran to our house. We

hurried up two flights of stairs to the attic. That's where our detective agency is.

Ashley opened her detective notebook and found the telephone number from the poster. She dialed the number, then pressed the speaker button on the phone so we could all hear.

The phone rang once. Twice. "Hello?" a woman answered. She sounded sad.

"Hello, my name is Ashley Olsen," my sister said. "Did you lose a cat named Lucy?"

"Yes! Did you find her?" the woman asked.

"No, not yet," Ashley said. "But we saw your sign. My sister, Mary-Kate, and I are detectives."

"Oh! I've heard of you two. You're the famous Trenchcoat Twins!" the woman cried. "My name is Mrs. Biddle. Will you help me find my Lucy?"

"Sure we will," Ashley said. "When did you last see her?"

"Last night. Lucy likes to stay outside at night. But every morning at seven o'clock she comes to my back door for her breakfast. This morning she didn't come. That's not like Lucy. Then at lunchtime Lucy didn't show up again. She's never done that before. I'm afraid she's gone for good!"

"Where does Lucy go at night?" Ashley asked.

"Lucy loves to wander around the neighborhood," Mrs. Biddle said. "She always visits the grocer, the fire station, and the little boy down the street."

Ashley wrote the list of places in her detective notebook.

"What does Lucy look like?" Ashley asked. She likes to get all the facts. That's what makes her a good detective.

"Lucy is quite unusual," Mrs. Biddle said.

"She's a large black cat. And she has a special white mark on her neck. Some people think the mark looks like a tattoo of a jack-o'-lantern."

"Is your cat a lucky cat?" I blurted out. I had to know!

Mrs. Biddle laughed. "Lucy has always brought me luck....Oh, girls, you have to find her! I miss Lucy so much!"

"We will," Ashley and I promised.

"What happens now?" Jane asked after Ashley hung up.

"Well, we know that Lucy likes to go to the same three places every night." I pointed to Ashley's list. "After school tomorrow we should check out those places for clues. Maybe someone saw her."

"Can I come?" Jane asked.

"Sure," I said. I pulled my spelling book out of my backpack. "See you t-o-m-o-r-r-o-w."

• • •

"Mary-Kate! Did you and Ashley find the tattooed cat yet?" Samantha asked me at school the next morning.

Jane told all the kids in our class about the case. Everyone wanted us to find the tattooed cat.

"No, not yet," I told Samantha.

"Mary-Kate! Mary-Kate!" Ashley called.

I hurried over to her at her cubby. She handed me a piece of lined notebook paper. There was a message written on it in black pen. It read: I HAVE THE TATOOED CAT! MEET ME AT THE END OF MAYWOOD STREET TONIGHT AT 6:30!

MEETING WITH A CATNAPPER

3

"**D**o you know what this means?" Ashley whispered.

"Of course." I huddled closer so no one else could hear. "The tattooed cat isn't lost. She's been catnapped!"

"Catnapped?" Ashley asked.

"Yes! Lucy was kidnapped—stolen by somebody. But she's a cat, so she was *cat-napped!*"

"I wonder why someone would take Mrs.

Biddle's cat," Ashley said thoughtfully.

"I don't know," I said. "And why does the catnapper want to meet us if he or she knows we're on the case?"

"Mary-Kate, Ashley," Mrs. Shaw called from the front of the room. "Are you two going to join us today?"

I whirled around. All the others in the class were already sitting at their desks with their notebooks open.

"Sorry!" my sister and I both called.

We shoved our backpacks into our cubbies. As we hurried to our desks, I saw Ashley slip the note into her notebook.

"Let's talk later," she whispered to me.

At recess, Ashley spread the note open on her lap. Then she pulled her detective notebook and a pencil out of her pocket. "What clues can we find in the note?"

I studied the note again. "Whoever wrote

this is a bad speller. He or she spelled the word *tattooed* wrong! He left out a *t*."

"Good clue, Mary-Kate!" Ashley wrote BAD SPELLER in her notebook. Then she turned the catnapper's note over and held it up to the sun. The light shone through the lined paper.

"There are no stains or special marks on the paper," she said. "It's plain notebook paper. Everyone at school has this kind of paper. And the note was written in regular black pen."

"We can't tell whose handwriting it is either," I added. "It's written in all capital letters."

We both studied the note some more. Then I snapped my fingers.

"We do know one thing, though," I said. "Whoever left this note in your cubby must go to our school."

Ashley's blue eyes lit up. "Yes! The note

writer must be in our class too! How else would he or she know where my cubby is?"

Ashley wrote SUSPECT IN OUR CLASS.

"But there are twenty other kids besides us in our class!" I groaned. "How do we find out who sent the note?"

"Easy!" Ashley said. "We meet him or her at the end of Maywood Street tonight at six-thirty!"

"It's so quiet," I whispered.

Ashley, Jane, and I stood on Maywood Street. We brought Clue along to help sniff out clues. There was no sign of the person who wrote the note.

Ashley pointed down the street. "There are only two more houses on Maywood Street. It's a dead end."

"A dark dead end," Jane said. "I can't see anything." Her voice shook.

"Don't worry," I said. "Clue will keep us

safe. She's a very brave basset hound."

When Jane heard where we were going, she begged to come along. But I could tell she didn't really want to be here now. She was scared.

The wind shook the trees along the side of the street. The dry leaves rustled. I looked around. I knew where we were. The back door of Chessa's Candies opened onto the dead end of Maywood Street. We came here almost every day. But things looked spooky in the dark!

We headed down the alley toward Lake Avenue—toward the dead end.

"This is too scary," Jane said. Her teeth chattered.

"The catnapper isn't here," I said. "We should go."

Ashley looked at her watch. "It's just six-thirty. Maybe the catnapper is late. Let's wait a little longer."

CRASH!

I jumped. "Wh-What was that?"

Ashley peered into the darkness. "I can't see a thing." She pulled a flashlight out of her backpack and turned it on.

"I'm out of here!" Jane said. "I'm—uh—I'm late for dinner!" She turned and ran down the street.

CRASH! BOOM!

Clue barked and took off running down the alley.

"Come on!" Ashley cried. I ran with her.

Clue stopped in front of three large metal garbage cans at the end of the alley. Suddenly a squirrel poked its furry gray face out from behind one of the cans! Clue lunged, and the squirrel scampered away.

I petted Clue. "You're not doing a very good job of sniffing out clues today," I teased. "It was just a squirrel!"

"Hey, what's that?" Ashley asked. She

shone her flashlight on the ground in front of the garbage cans. Something shiny lay there.

I bent down and picked it up.

It was a baseball card! The gold hologram card that Zach got yesterday!

THE CATNAPPER'S CARD

"**Z**ach is the catnapper!" I said. "This card proves it."

Ashley pulled a plastic evidence bag from her backpack and slipped the baseball card into it.

"Finding Zach's baseball card here doesn't prove that he took the cat," she said.

"But it makes him a good suspect," I said. "And everyone knows that Zach is a bad speller."

"That's true," Ashley said slowly. "But a lot of kids are bad spellers...and a lot of kids collect baseball cards."

"I think we should talk to Zach tomorrow," I said.

Ashley nodded. She took out her detective notebook and wrote SUSPECT #1: ZACH JONES.

"Everybody line up," Mrs. Shaw said to our class the next morning. "Time for another practice spelling bee."

Half the class groaned. Not me. I was ready. After dinner last night I studied and studied my spelling words. I was a spelling machine!

I took one last look in my spelling book. Then I put the book back on my desk and hurried to the front of the room.

Zach was up first—and out first when he spelled a word wrong. Then Christy Gallo, Charlie Tinfow, George Clark, and Jane all

missed easy words and had to sit down. Ashley lasted until the second round before she missed a word. Finally only Samantha and I were left.

"Mary-Kate," Mrs. Shaw said, "your word is *phantom*."

I sounded out the word. "F-a-n-t-o-m," I spelled.

Mrs. Shaw shook her head. "I'm sorry, Mary-Kate. That is not right."

It was Samantha's turn. She spelled it right—"p-h-a-n-t-o-m"—and won again!

I was upset. I wanted to find the tattooed cat more than ever! I knew it was the only sure way I could win the school spelling bee.

The bell rang for lunch. "Let's go talk to Zach," I said.

In the lunchroom Ashley and I marched right up to a group of boys trading baseball cards.

"Zach," I said, "we need to talk to you."

Ashley pulled the gold hologram card out of the plastic bag. She waved it in front of Zach's nose. "Is this yours?"

George Clark grabbed the card right out of Ashley's hand. "Hey! Where did you find my card?" he asked.

"On Maywood Street behind the candy store. But we thought it was Zach's card," I said.

Zach shook his head. "It used to be mine. But I traded it to George."

I put my hands on my hips. "But you said this card was really rare. You wouldn't trade it to Tim for five cards!"

Zachary smiled. "I changed my mind after I got *another* gold hologram card. Can you believe it? Two in one day! How lucky is that? And George gave me ten cards for the one I traded him. *Ten* cards!"

George pushed his curly black hair out

of his eyes and nodded. "Yup. But I lost it right after Zach gave it to me."

Ashley and I looked at each other. Was George telling us the truth? Or was he the catnapper?

"Did you leave a note in my cubby yesterday?" Ashley asked George.

George turned red. "No way!" he said. "I don't write notes to girls!"

The other boys giggled.

Ashley and I took off across the lunchroom and sat down at a table. Ashley pulled out her detective notebook.

"I think we should add George to our list," she said. "He could have been lying."

"You're right. George is also a bad speller. He gets a lot of easy words wrong," I said.

Ashley wrote SUSPECT #2: GEORGE CLARK. She tapped the pencil against the page. "We have to keep Zach on the list. The card we found could have been his. So now we have two suspects."

"And we still don't know why the cat-napper didn't show up last night," I pointed out.

"I know," Ashley said. "We have a lot more detective work to do."

"And I have a lot more studying to do." I opened my spelling book.

A piece of notebook paper fluttered to the floor.

"Hey, Mary-Kate, you dropped something," Ashley said. She picked it up and gave it to me.

"This isn't mine," I said. I looked at the note and gasped. "It's another note from the catnapper!"

"What does the note say?" Ashley asked.

I showed it to her. It read: MEET ME AT THE GRAVEYARD TOMORROW AT 6:30 IF YOU WANT THE TATOOED CAT!

"The graveyard?" I turned to Ashley. "Why does the catnapper want to meet us at the graveyard?"

Ashley shook her head. "It's weird, all right." She took the note and looked at it closely. "It's the same lined notebook paper. The same black pen. The same capital letters. And the same spelling mistake! So the same person wrote both notes."

"And I still have the same questions," I said. "Why does the catnapper keep writing to us? Why would he or she want to give us the tattooed cat?"

"The catnapper is up to something," Ashley said. "We're going to have to meet him or her to find out what it is."

"How do we know this is for real?" I asked. "Maybe someone is playing tricks on us. Maybe it's all a joke to scare us."

"What's a joke?" Jane came up behind us. Ashley showed her the note.

"We have no choice," Ashley told me. "Good detectives follow every lead. We have to go to the graveyard tomorrow night." She turned to Jane. "Do you want to come with us?"

Jane bit her lip. "I know I said I wanted to help. But I didn't think it would be so scary. I'm done being a detective."

I turned to my sister. "I don't want to go to a graveyard at night either! Do we really have to?"

ANOTHER SCARY NIGHT

"I can't believe you talked me into this," I said to Ashley the next night.

The graveyard was even spookier than I thought it would be. An owl hooted. I jumped and turned on my flashlight.

"Do you think the catnapper will show up tonight?" Ashley asked. She held Clue's leash as Clue sniffed the damp ground.

Crunch! Crunch!

"What's that?" I shined my flashlight on

the crumbling old gravestones. "Footsteps! Someone's here."

We stopped walking and listened.

Crunch! Crunch!

"Who's there?" Ashley called into the darkness.

There was no answer. We listened harder. A few seconds later, we heard someone running.

"Let's go after him!" Ashley said. She and Clue raced off.

No way was I staying behind! I ran after them.

We dodged around the gravestones. Clue led the way. We ran and ran. Then the footsteps stopped.

Ashley pulled on Clue's leash. We stood together and listened. The only sound was our huffing and puffing.

"We lost him," I said. I moved the flashlight back and forth. We were now at the far end of the graveyard, near a fence.

Suddenly there was a rustling behind us. Then we heard a loud hissing noise.

I whirled around—and dropped the flashlight. It hit the ground with a loud *thump* and went off.

In the darkness I saw a pair of yellow eyes staring right at us!

I stood frozen in my tracks. *What was it? Was it going to attack?*

Clue growled from deep in her throat. She pulled at her leash.

Ashley reached down and grabbed the flashlight. She flicked it on.

I sighed with relief. It was just a raccoon!

The raccoon turned and raced off into the night.

Ashley shone the flashlight onto the path in front of us. "I wonder why the catnapper ran away again."

I didn't know—and in the dark, spooky

graveyard, I didn't care. I tugged Ashley's arm. "Let's go home."

"Wait, Mary-Kate," Ashley said. "I see something." She aimed her flashlight at the grave behind us. We inched closer. Something was there.

I reached down and picked it up.

"It's a pet collar!" Ashley studied the tag attached to the collar. "Look—Mrs. Biddle's name and address are on the tag!"

I looked at the tag. "It's Lucy's collar, all right. But why did the catnapper bring us here and then run away and leave us Lucy's collar?"

"I don't know," Ashley said. "But at least we now know that whoever wrote the notes really does have Lucy."

"Look!" I pointed to the ground near the gravestone. "There's another note." I snatched it up.

We read: THE TATOOED CAT WILL BE AT 1313

ELM STREET TOMORROW NIGHT!

"1313 Elm Street?" Ashley asked. "Isn't that—"

A chill went up my spine. I knew that address. All the kids at school knew that address.

"That's the address of the haunted house!"

S-U-S-P-E-C-T

"It's just an empty old house," Ashley said. "It's not haunted."

We sat upstairs in our attic office drinking hot chocolate. Clue slept on the rug. She was tired from our chase through the graveyard.

"How do you know that?" I asked. "Everyone at school says it's haunted."

"I know because there is no such thing as a haunted house!" Ashley said.

"That's what you said about the tattooed

cat, remember?" I said. "But now we know that Lucy is real."

Ashley smiled. "Okay, you got me there. I guess we'll just have to go see if the house really is haunted."

"Whoa! I'm not going into a haunted house!" I yanked open my spelling book and stared down at the page.

Ashley didn't give up. "Mary-Kate," she said, "we just got a new clue. The clue leads us to that house. We have to follow the clue. That's what Great-grandma Olive would do."

I sighed. Ashley was right. Our Great-grandma Olive is a famous detective. She taught us everything we know about solving mysteries. She wouldn't be scared off a case by a haunted house.

I stared at the notes spread out on the desk. If we solved the case soon, we wouldn't have to go to the haunted house.

"I know!" I pointed to the second note. "Someone put that note in my spelling book. The only time I didn't have my spelling book was during the spelling bee. I left it on my desk. That means someone put the note inside my book during the spelling bee—someone who was out in the first round. You were out in the second, and you would have seen if someone put the note in because you sit next to me."

Ashley's eyes sparkled. "Good thinking, Mary-Kate!" She flipped open her notebook. "Zach was out the first round, and so was George."

I thought back to the spelling bee. "Christy, Jane, and Charlie were out in the first round too."

Ashley wrote down all their names. "Now we have *five* suspects!"

"That's too many," I said. "We have to rule some of them out." I reached over her shoulder and flipped through the notebook pages. "I got it!"

"What?" Ashley asked. "What?"

"Do you need me to *spell* it out for you?" I asked with a grin.

Ashley gazed down at the notes.

"The spelling mistake!" she cried. "The catnapper made the same spelling mistake in all three notes. He or she spelled the word *tattooed* wrong—without three *t*'s."

"That's how we'll catch him," I said. "Tomorrow we'll get all five suspects to spell *tattooed*. Whoever spells it wrong, without three *t*'s, is the person who wrote the notes."

"Do you think it will work?" Ashley asked.

"It better," I said, crossing my fingers. "If we catch the catnapper tomorrow, we won't have to go to the haunted house!"

TATTOO YOU

The next day at school, right before lunch, Mrs. Shaw said, "For the next twenty minutes we will all study for the big spelling bee. Quiz one another—quietly."

I gave Ashley a thumbs-up. It was the perfect time to put our plan into action!

We hurried over to Zach.

"Hey, Zach," Ashley said, "Mary-Kate and I don't know how to spell the word *tattooed*. Can you help us?"

Zach looked confused. "You two are asking *me* how to spell something? But I'm really bad at spelling."

"You're not that bad," I said with a smile. "Can't you just try? Please?"

"Sure," Zach said with a shrug. "T-a-t-o-o-e-d."

"That's great!" I cried.

Ashley circled Zach's name in her notebook. Zach was now a big-time suspect. I was sure we would have this case solved in no time!

"You guys sure are acting weird," Zach called as we hurried over to George's desk.

George spelled the word wrong too—the same way Zach did. Ashley put a circle around his name too.

Next we asked Charlie to spell it. "No problem," he said. "T-a-t-t-o-e-d."

Charlie spelled it wrong, but not the same way as the note writer. He left out

one *o*. Ashley crossed his name off our list.

"Where's Christy?" I asked Ashley. I looked around the room. Everyone sat in groups spelling words aloud.

"Near the window, next to Samantha." Ashley pointed to the girl in the pink shirt. We hurried over to her.

"Hey, can you guys spell *tattooed*?" I asked.

"Sure," Samantha said.

I rolled my eyes. Of course *Samantha* could spell it!

Ashley jumped in. "What about you, Christy?"

"T-a-t-t-o-o-e-d," Christy spelled.

"Great job," I said. Christy spelled it right! She was not the note writer. Ashley put a line through Christy's name.

Jane walked by. "Jane, can you spell *tattooed*?" Ashley called out.

Jane smiled. Then she spelled it the

wrong way—the same way it was spelled in the notes!

I followed Ashley to her desk. Ashley circled Jane's name. Now she was a suspect too.

"Do you really think it could be Jane?" I asked. "After all, she was helping us with the case."

"I know, but she did spell the word wrong." Ashley looked at the circled names and frowned. "So now we have three suspects. And no more clues."

"Lunchtime," Mrs. Shaw called.

I groaned. The case wasn't even close to being solved. Now I knew we would *have* to go to the haunted house!

8

THE HAUNTED HOUSE

Ashley and I stared up at the house at 1313 Elm Street. No one had lived in the house for as long as I could remember.

Most of the windows were broken. Some were boarded up. Weeds had sprouted all over the lawn.

Clue whined.

"See, Ashley? Even Clue doesn't want to go in there," I said.

"Let's just peek in a window," Ashley

said, "and see if anyone is inside."

"Really fast, okay?" I said.

I followed Ashley slowly up the cracked front path to a window by the front door. We pressed our faces up against the dirty glass. The living room was dark and empty. Cobwebs hung from the ceiling.

Ashley turned toward the door. I grabbed her arm and squeezed it tightly.

"No way," I said. "Tim told me that people who go into this house never, ever come out."

Ashley looked at me. Her blue eyes were wide and her face was white. "I—I think you're right, Mary-Kate. There's no one here. Let's go."

Then we heard something.

Clue perked up and started to sniff the air.

I looked at Ashley. "Did you hear something?"

Meow. Meow.

Ashley straightened her shoulders and reached for the doorknob. "Come on, Mary-Kate. It sounds like a cat. We have to check it out."

Ashley pushed open the front door. The hinges creaked loudly.

We stepped inside the haunted house.

The wooden floor was covered with thick dust. I gripped Clue's leash tightly as Ashley reached inside her backpack. She pulled out two flashlights and handed one to me.

"Let's call for the cat from here," I said.

"Here, kitty, kitty," called Ashley. "Here, Lucy!" Her voice echoed in the empty house.

Creeaak!

"What was that?" I asked.

Creeaak! Bam!

"Not a cat," Ashley whispered, her eyes wide. "I think there's someone here."

Creeaak! Bam!

I shone my flashlight in front of me. The strange noise was coming from the back of the house.

"O-Only ghosts make noises like that," I told my sister.

"We've come this far," Ashley said. "We have to check it out."

We walked down a hallway and into a room that looked like the kitchen. An old rusted stove stood in one corner of the room. Suddenly a large, dark shadow loomed over us!

Creeaak! Bam!

"Run!" I screamed.

"Wait, Mary-Kate!" Ashley pulled me back. "It's just a swinging door." She pointed to a wooden pantry door. "The wind is making this door swing and creak."

Creeaak! Bam!

I watched the door. Ashley was right. As

the door moved, it creaked and slammed and made shadows. I opened the door all the way to stop it from swinging.

Everything got quiet. Then we heard something.

Meow. Meow.

"Where is that meowing coming from?" Ashley asked.

Clue sniffed the air. Then she pulled me toward a large staircase.

"Upstairs," I said.

We crept up the stairs slowly. Each stair groaned under our weight. The wood looked rotten. I hoped it wouldn't break. I held Ashley's hand as we climbed. What was waiting for us at the top?

I was afraid to find out.

We reached the top stair and stopped. Three doors led off a hallway. They were all open.

Then we heard a faint *meow* coming

from the farthest room. We followed Clue to the room. Thick cobwebs brushed my face as we entered.

Something leaped at us from out of the darkness!

Ashley dropped her flashlight and screamed. I jumped.

"Ashley! Are you all right? What is it?" I shone my flashlight on her.

Sitting in Ashley's arms was a cat—a black cat!

Ashley took a deep breath and let it out slowly.

I hurried over. "Does it have a tattoo? Is it Lucy?" I cried.

My flashlight lit up the cat's black fur. Yes! There was a white jack-o'-lantern tattoo on the cat's neck!

"We found the tattooed cat! Case closed!" I yelled.

Clue barked.

Ashley stroked the cat, calming her down. The cat began to purr softly.

"Let's take Lucy home," I said. "We have to call Mrs. Biddle right away."

We rushed downstairs and out the front door. At the corner of Elm, we waited to cross the street. The light changed, and I took off. But Ashley didn't move.

"What's wrong?" I asked.

Ashley looked at her hand and frowned. "Mary-Kate, this isn't the right cat. This isn't Lucy."

"What?" I cried. "Of course it's the right cat. How many cats have jack-o'-lantern tattoos?"

"I'm telling you," Ashley said, "this is *not* the right cat."

9

THE WRONG CAT

Ashley showed me her hand. Her fingers were covered with white paint. "Someone painted this cat."

"Huh?" I looked closely at the cat's neck. The white jack-o'-lantern tattoo was smeared!

"This cat does not have a tattoo," Ashley said. "But someone wanted us to think it does."

"Why would someone paint a cat?" I

asked. "Who would do such a thing?"

"I don't know," Ashley said. "But this case keeps getting stranger and stranger. This is the third time the catnapper sent us a note to meet him but didn't show up."

"Let me see that cat," I said. I took the cat in my arms and scratched her behind the ears. She purred.

"This cat is no stray. She's clean and fat. And she's really sweet," I said. "This cat belongs to someone!"

"Yes, but who?" Ashley asked.

I looked at the cat's neck. "She has a collar but no tag. Someone took off the tag with the owner's name and address on it."

"Maybe this cat belongs to the catnapper," Ashley said. "Maybe the catnapper painted this cat so we would think it was Lucy and bring her back to Mrs. Biddle. Then we would stop searching, and the catnapper would get to keep the real tattooed cat."

We continued down the street. The street was empty, so I let Clue off her leash. Clue knew her way home. She trotted a few steps ahead of us.

Watching Clue gave me a great idea!

"Hey, Ashley," I said, "remember last summer when Dad left Clue at the park by mistake?"

Ashley nodded.

"And remember how Clue found her own way home?" I said. "Maybe this cat can do the same thing!"

"Let's try it!" Ashley said.

I put the cat down on the ground. She looked around, then raced down the street. Ashley, Clue, and I ran after her. The cat turned down Maple Street.

Clue barked and sprinted ahead of us. She was right behind the cat. The cat darted under a clump of bushes and into a backyard. Clue stayed on her trail.

In and out of backyards, around trees, and under bushes, Clue chased the cat. We chased Clue. Every few minutes Clue let out a loud bark to let us know where she was.

Ashley and I followed Clue to the corner of Maple Street and Oak Place. Clue sat on the curb. She panted and looked confused. The cat was nowhere to be seen.

Ashley pushed her strawberry-blond hair out of her eyes. We were both out of breath from running so fast.

"We lost the cat!" she cried. "Now what do we do?"

I leaned forward and whispered into Clue's floppy ear, "Find the cat, Clue."

Clue sniffed my hands. The cat's smell was still on my skin. "Clue's the best sniffer around," I said. "She won't let us down."

Clue sniffed to the left. Then she sniffed to the right. Then she ran down Oak Place.

"Clue is back on the trail!" I cheered.

Ashley and I followed our dog. Halfway down the road Clue put her nose to the ground and crossed a yard. She led us up to a blue house.

Sitting by the front door was the black cat! She was scratching on the door.

The door opened. The cat jumped into a boy's arms.

Ashley and I gasped.

It was George Clark!

10

GIVE A HUG

"**G**eorge!" I cried. I couldn't stop myself.

George looked surprised to see me and Ashley and Clue in his front yard.

"Hi! What are you two doing here?" he asked.

"We were wondering," Ashley said, "is that your cat?" She pointed to the cat purring softly in his arms.

"Yeah," George said. "This is Misty. Why?"

"Are you the one who painted a jack-o'-lantern on your cat?" I asked.

"Paint my cat? Are you nuts?" Then George looked down at Misty. He saw the white paint smeared all over her black fur. "Yuck! I didn't do that!"

"Do you know what Misty was doing inside the haunted house?" Ashley asked.

George scratched his head. "I didn't even know Misty had left our yard."

I looked George right in the eye. "Are you the catnapper?" I asked. "Did you take Lucy, the tattooed cat?"

"No!" George said.

We stared at George and Misty, trying to decide if we should believe him or not.

Ashley looked closely at Misty. "She's a sweet cat."

George smiled. "Thanks."

"Can I give her a hug good-bye?" Ashley asked.

I stared at my sister. I had a feeling she was up to something.

"Sure," George said. He handed Misty to Ashley.

Ashley gave Misty a quick hug. Misty purred.

Then Ashley said, "We've got to get home. See you in school tomorrow." She pushed Misty into George's arms and grabbed my hand. We hurried home with Clue.

Upstairs in our attic office I turned to my sister. "Okay, why did you want to hug Misty?"

"Because I wanted to grab this!" Ashley wrapped a tissue around her hand and reached into her backpack. She pulled out Misty's collar. "Look! What do you see?"

I looked closely at the collar. At first I saw only a smudge of white paint on it. Then I took a better look. It wasn't a smudge. It was a fingerprint—a thumbprint!

I could tell it was a thumbprint because it was bigger than other fingerprints

"It could be one of our thumbprints," I told Ashley.

"I know," Ashley said. She placed the collar on my desk. "But it could also be the catnapper's print."

Our Great-grandma Olive taught us all about fingerprinting. Fingerprints help her solve lots of cases.

I opened one of my desk drawers. I pulled out two small cards. Ashley and I keep our fingerprints on file—just in case.

I grabbed a magnifying glass from the top of the desk. I looked at the pattern of the thumbprint on the collar. Then I looked at our thumbprints. They were different.

"This *is* the catnapper's print!" I exclaimed.

Ashley opened her notebook. "We have

three suspects—Zach, George, and Jane. They all spelled the word *tattooed* wrong. All we have to do now is get their thumbprints. Whoever's print matches the one on Misty's collar stole the tattooed cat!"

I gave Ashley a high five. Soon we would catch the catnapper!

~The New Adventures of~ MARY-KATE & ASHLEY ™

DETECTIVE TRICK

FACTS ABOUT FINGERPRINTS

Did you know that no two people in the world have the same fingerprints? Even identical twins! And your fingerprints never change—they stay the same as you get older. That's why finding a fingerprint at the scene of a crime is one of the best ways in which a detective can catch a guilty person.

Even though everyone's fingerprints are different, there are three main types of fingerprint patterns. Which pattern do your fingerprints look like?

1. The Arch: the shape in the middle looks like an arch.

2. The Loop: the shape in the middle looks like a loop.

3. The Whorl: the shape in the middle looks like lines in a circle.

From
The Case Of The TATTOOED CAT

mary-kateandashley.com
America Online Keyword: mary-kateandashley

~The New Adventures of~ MARY-KATE & ASHLEY ™

GATHERING CLUES

When the Trenchcoat Twins investigate a mystery, they always keep an eye out for clues that will help them solve the case. When they find a clue, they make sure to handle it very carefully. Here are some tips on how to gather clues:

- You will need a pair of tweezers and a plastic bag that is big enough to hold the clue.

- Use the tweezers to pick up the clue and place it in the bag. Be careful not to touch it with your fingers, or you might leave your own fingerprints!

- For each clue that you find, write down the following information: where you found the clue, when you found it, and what you think it means.

- Don't let anyone else touch it!

Look for our next mystery . . .
The Case Of The Nutcracker Ballet

mary-kateandashley.com
America Online Keyword: mary-kateandashley

DIRTY FINGERS

Operation Fingerprint started at lunch-time.

We waited for our whole class to enter the cafeteria. Ashley and I found a table by ourselves across the room from our friends.

"George first," I whispered.

Ashley opened her backpack and took out our fingerprinting supplies. Then she pulled a chocolate cupcake covered with gobs of white icing out of a box. She held the cupcake in one hand and an opened can of soda wrapped in a paper napkin in the other.

"You ready?" she asked.

I pulled out three sheets of white paper and a roll of clear tape. I lined up my paint-brushes on the table. Then I opened a packet of hot-chocolate mix.

"Go for it!" I said.

Ashley marched to George's table. He was sitting with Tim. They were close enough so that I could hear everything.

"Hi, George," Ashley said. "I wanted to say I'm sorry for bothering you and Misty last night. So I baked you this yummy cup-cake."

She pushed the cupcake into George's hand.

George looked surprised. "Thanks!" he said.

"Aren't you going to eat it?" Ashley asked.

George took a big bite. The icing oozed over his fingers. Before he could finish chewing, Ashley pushed the can of soda toward him. "Have a drink to wash it down."

George grabbed the can and took a big gulp. Ashley quickly snatched the can back with her napkin. "Got to go."

She hurried back to me. George stared after her, scratching his head. He looked totally confused! I tried not to giggle.

Ashley placed the soda can on the table. I could see the sticky white thumbprint on the side. It was my job to lift the print off the can. I got to work.

First I sprinkled some hot-chocolate powder on the print. Then I gently brushed it with a paintbrush to get rid of the extra powder. Next I took a piece of tape and placed the sticky side on the print. Slowly I

lifted the tape and placed the print on the white paper.

Ashley wrote *George* next to the thumbprint with a pencil. "One down. Two to go," she said.

She pulled another cupcake out of her backpack and unwrapped the foil. This cupcake also had tons of sticky icing. Then she opened another can of soda. The smooth, shiny can was a perfect surface for collecting fingerprints.

She walked over to Zach's table. She gave him the sticky cupcake and the soda—just like she did with George. As soon as Zach's thumbprint was on the can, she hurried over to me.

Ashley carefully placed the can on the table. I got to work. Soon I had Zach's thumbprint on a piece of paper.

"What about Jane?" I asked. "I don't think she will eat a messy cupcake."

"I have another way to get her finger-print," Ashley said. She took an ink pad and a thin marker out of her backpack. She reached for my last sheet of white paper.

"I need to use this," she said. "Come with me and follow what I do. Okay?"

"Okay," I said.

Ashley and I sat down with Jane and Samantha.

"Anyone know how to make fingerprint art?" Ashley asked. "I can make a cool snow-man using my thumb and this ink pad. See?"

I watched Ashley make three thumb-prints—one above the other. She drew a face on the top one with the marker.

"Why don't you try, Jane?" Ashley asked.

Jane pressed her thumb onto the ink pad. She made three marks on the paper. She drew a face on her snowman.

"I know," Jane said. "I can draw arms and legs and buttons too."

Before she had the chance, Ashley snatched away the paper. "Art lesson is over," she said with a smile. Then she grabbed my hand and we hurried back to our table.

Operation Fingerprint was a success!

We rushed home after school. Upstairs in our attic we laid all three sheets of paper on my desk. We took out Misty's collar. It was time to compare prints. Who was the catnapper?

I pulled out the magnifying glass. George was first. I peered closely. "Nope! His thumbprint doesn't match," I said.

Zach was next. "Nope!" I said.

Ashley and I looked at each other. Jane must be the catnapper! To be sure, I compared Jane's thumbprint to the one we found on Misty's collar.

"It's a match!" I said. "Let's go talk to Jane!"

12

LOST AND FOUND

Ashley and I hopped onto our bikes and pedaled to Jane's house. I still couldn't believe it was Jane. She wanted to help us *solve* the case! But all the evidence pointed to her.

Jane answered the door right away. "Hi, guys! What are you doing here?"

"We know you're the catnapper," I said.

Ashley showed Jane the thumbprint on Misty's collar and how it matched the one

she got from her at lunchtime.

Jane hung her head. "It was me," she confessed. "I took Lucy."

"But why did you steal her?" Ashley asked.

"I didn't *steal* her—I found her!" Jane said. "I found her right before I met you guys at Chessa's Candies. I brought her home. I was going to take her back to her owner. Mrs. Biddle's name was on the tag."

"So why didn't you?" Ashley asked.

"I was going to tell you about it," Jane said, "but then I heard you talking about the lucky cat—"

"And you wanted to keep the cat until Halloween so you could get a wish to come true," I guessed.

Jane nodded. She looked embarrassed. "I really want to win the spelling bee."

"Me too!" I said.

"So when I found out you two were

going to look for the missing cat, I realized I had to do everything I could to keep you from finding her right away," Jane said.

"You wrote the notes," Ashley said. "You sent us on a chase to nowhere!"

"I had to keep you off my trail," Jane explained. "I even borrowed George's cat and put her in the haunted house."

"*And* you painted her!" I cried.

"I'm sorry." Jane looked down. "I guess I should apologize to George too."

We heard a soft meow. Lucy, the real tattooed cat, came into the room. She walked up to Jane and nuzzled her leg.

I reached down to pet Lucy. She purred.

"Lucy's owner misses her a lot," I said. "She's very sad."

Jane nodded. "It was wrong of me to keep her."

"Can we use your telephone?" Ashley asked.

"Sure. But why?" Jane pointed to the phone at the end of the front hall.

"It's time to call Mrs. Biddle and tell her Lucy is safe." Ashley picked up the phone and began to dial.

Three days later, I stood on the huge stage in the school auditorium. I waved to my family and to Mrs. Biddle in the audience.

Mrs. Biddle was so happy when we brought Lucy home on Halloween. She let me pet Lucy and make my wish.

Now as I stood on the stage, I licked my lips and waited for my next turn. Would my wish come true? Was Lucy really a lucky cat?

The principal spoke into the microphone. "Ladies and gentlemen, we are down to our last two spellers—Mary-Kate Olsen and Samantha Samuels."

He pulled a card from his pile. "Samantha, your word is *disguise*."

Samantha stepped forward into the bright lights. She took a deep breath. "Disguise. D-i-s-g-e-y-e-s."

"I'm sorry, that is incorrect," the principal said.

I stepped forward. I looked to the side of the stage. Ashley smiled at me from the wings.

I smiled back, took a deep breath, and spelled: "D-i-s-g-u-i-s-e."

The next thing I heard was the principal saying, "Our new school spelling bee champion is Mary-Kate Olsen!"

I jumped up and down and hugged Samantha. The principal placed a medal around my neck. I rushed into the wings and hugged Ashley.

"See? Lucy really is lucky!" I said. "I made a wish to win the spelling bee and I won!"

"You won because you studied nonstop," Ashley said. "The cat didn't make you win. You did it yourself."

"I did study a lot," I said slowly. "But I still think Lucy brings good luck."

Ashley said, "There's no such thing as a lucky cat."

"Yes, there is!"

"No, there isn't!"

Ashley and I grinned at each other.

"Wait until next year," I said. "I'll pet Lucy again on Halloween and make another wish, and when my wish comes true that will prove that she's lucky."

Ashley laughed. "Okay, we'll try it again next year," she said.

Hi from both of us,

Ashley and I couldn't wait for opening night of the Nutcracker Ballet. Ashley was dancing the role of a party guest. I would get to wear a red velvet uniform and show people to their seats at the performance. And our good friend, Miranda, was dancing the lead role of Clara!

The day before the performance, someone stole Miranda's lucky ballet slippers!

Want to find out what happened? Check out the next page for a sneak peek at *The New Adventures of Mary-Kate & Ashley*: The Case Of The Nutcracker Ballet.

See you next time!

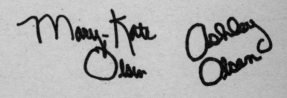

The Case Of The
Nutcracker Ballet

"Ashley, you're dancing in the Nutcracker Ballet tomorrow!" I said to my twin sister. "You're practically famous!"

I was sitting with Ashley and our friend, Samantha, in a corner of Madame Pavlova's dance studio. Ashley's ballet class practiced there every week. And tomorrow they would perform in the Pavlova Theater, right next door!

"Come on, Mary-Kate." Ashley blushed. "I have a *small* part in the ballet. But I love being in the show."

"Are you nervous, Ashley?" Samantha asked. She was thinking about joining

Ashley's dance class next year. Madame Pavlova said she could watch the rehearsal.

"Well, maybe a little," Ashley admitted. She tightened the ribbons on her ballet slippers. "But I'll feel better once we get to practice onstage with our costumes."

"Dancers, take your places please." Madame Pavlova clapped her hands.

Madame Pavlova had pale smooth skin and big brown eyes. Her black hair was wrapped tightly in a bun. "I want to run through the Christmas party dance before we go to the theater," she said. "And I want no mistakes this time!"

"Wow," Samantha said. "Madame P. is pretty tough."

"She's strict," I said, "but she's a great teacher. Right, Ashley?"

"She's the best," Ashley said. "See you guys later!"

Ashley rushed to join the other dancers in the center of the room. She did a perfect twirl when she reached her spot on the floor.

Samantha and I are helping out with the ballet. We're going to be ushers tomorrow at the performance. We'll get to wear red velvet uniforms and show people to their seats.

"Okay." Madame Pavlova turned on the music. "And . . . begin."

Ashley and the other girls and boys began dancing their roles. They pretended to be at a Christmas party. A girl named Miranda danced through the center of the crowd. Miranda was the star of the ballet. She played the role of Clara.

Miranda twirled with her arms above her head. She lifted her leg high and—

"Ow!" Miranda cried. She fell to the floor.

Madame Pavlova stopped the music. "You must *concentrate*, Miranda," she said. "I can't have you falling onstage tomorrow."

A girl named Becky giggled. "I told you she dances like an elephant," she said.

"Maybe *I* should play Clara."

"You pushed me!" Miranda cried.

"Did not!" Becky said.

"Did too!" Miranda replied.

"Quiet!" Madame Pavlova put a hand to her forehead. "There will be no fighting in my ballet, no horsing around, and no talking! Or *nobody* will dance tomorrow. Let's begin again," she said.

After the practice was over, Samantha and I joined Ashley by the water fountain just outside the studio.

"Becky did push me," Miranda was saying. "But I don't care. Madame Pavlova knows I'm a good dancer. And I'm going to do great tomorrow."

"You're always so sure of yourself," Ashley said. "What's your secret?"

Miranda smiled. "I'm going to wear my lucky ballet slippers."

Miranda's ballet slippers were no secret.

Everybody knew about them—even me. Miranda wears them for every performance. They're supposed to help her dance her best.

"Everybody's going to be awesome," Samantha said. "I can't wait to see the dress rehearsal."

"Do you guys need help with your costumes?" I asked. I knew Ashley's dress had a tricky zipper.

"Thanks, Mary-Kate," Ashley said. "Let's go."

We skipped down the hall to the girls' dressing room. Everyone was buzzing with excitement.

"I'll see you guys in a few minutes." Miranda squeezed her way to her cubby at the back of the dressing room.

"You looked awesome out there, Ashley!" Samantha said once Ashley was in her costume. "How long have you been dancing?"

Ashley was about to answer, when we heard a terrible scream. It was Miranda!

"Oh, no!" Miranda cried. "My lucky ballet slippers. Somebody stole my lucky ballet slippers!"

mary-kate and ashley

ourstory

The OFFICIAL Biography

8-page color photo insert

You've seen them on television and in the movies. Now see them up close and personal!

In *Our Story*, Mary-Kate and Ashley give you the real deal on:

- Being teen stars!
- Their big break in show biz!
- What happens behind the scenes on their movies and television series!
- Their careers as designers!
- Secret crushes! (Shhh...)
- Their hopes and dreams for the future!
- And so much more!

Coming soon wherever books are sold!

Revised and updated! Plus never-before-seen photos!

Win a Camp Survival Kit!

Everything you need for a fabulous summer of fun!

Survive the Summer in Style!

Grand Prize includes:

- A set of 4 autographed camp-themed books from *The New Adventures of Mary-Kate & Ashley* book series

- Backpack, personal CD player, sunglasses, music CDs, and more from **the mary-kateandashley brand**

- Journal, pens, address book, stationery and postage stamps

THE NEW ADVENTURES OF MARY-KATE & ASHLEY™
Camp Survival Kit Sweepstakes

OFFICIAL RULES:

1. No purchase necessary.

2. To enter complete the official entry form or hand print your name, address, age, and phone number along with the w[ords] "THE NEW ADVENTURES OF MARY-KATE & ASHLEY Camp Survival Kit Sweepstakes" on a 3" x 5" card and mail [to] THE NEW ADVENTURES OF MARY-KATE & ASHLEY Camp Survival Kit Sweepstakes, c/o HarperEntertainment, Attn: Children's Marke[ting] Department, 10 East 53rd Street, New York, NY 10022. Entries must be received no later than October 31, 2003. Enter as ofte[n as] you wish, but each entry must be mailed separately. One entry per envelope. Partially completed, illegible, or mechani[cally] reproduced entries will not be accepted. Sponsors are not responsible for lost, late, mutilated, illegible, stolen, postage [due,] incomplete, or misdirected entries. All entries become the property of Dualstar Entertainment Group, LLC, and will not be returne[d.]

3. Sweepstakes open to all legal residents of the United States (excluding Colorado and Rhode Island), who are between the age[s of] five and fifteen on October 31, 2003, excluding employees and immediate family members of HarperCollins Publishers, ("HarperCollins"), Parachute Properties and Parachute Press, Inc., and their respective subsidiaries and affiliates, officers, direc[tors,] shareholders, employees, agents, attorneys, and other representatives (individually and collectively "Parachute"), Dua[lstar] Entertainment Group, LLC, and its subsidiaries and affiliates, officers, directors, shareholders, employees, agents, attorneys, and o[ther] representatives (individually and collectively "Dualstar"), and their respective parent companies, affiliates, subsidia[ries,] advertising, promotion and fulfillment agencies, and the persons with whom each of the above are domiciled. Offer void w[here] prohibited or restricted by law.

4. Odds of winning depend on the total number of entries received. Approximately 400,000 sweepstakes announcements publis[hed.] All prizes will be awarded. Winners will be randomly drawn on or about November 15, 2003, by HarperCollins, whose deci[sions] are final. Potential winner will be notified by mail and will be required to sign and return an affidavit of eligibility and relea[se of] liability within 14 days of notification. Prizes won by minors will be awarded to parent or legal guardian who must sign and r[eturn] all required legal documents. By acceptance of the prize, winner consents to the use of his or her name, photograph, like[ness] and biographical information by HarperCollins, Parachute, Dualstar, and for publicity purposes without further compensation e[xcept] where prohibited.

5. One (1) Grand Prize Winner wins a Camp Survival Kit to include the following items: a backpack, personal CD player, sungla[sses,] photo frame and three music CDs from the *mary-kateandashley* brand; a hat, stationery, a journal, three pens, 20 first-[class] postage stamps, an address book; one autographed copy of each of the following books from THE NEW ADVENTURE[S OF] MARY-KATE & ASHLEY book series: THE CASE OF THE SUMMER CAMP CAPER, THE CASE OF THE CHEERLEADING CAMP MYST[ERY,] THE CASE OF THE DOG CAMP MYSTERY, and THE CASE OF CAMP CROOKED LAKE. Approximate retail value: $210.00.

6. Only one prize will be awarded per individual, family, or household. Prizes are non-transferable and cannot be substituted, s[old or] redeemed for cash. Any federal, state, or local taxes are the responsibility of the winner. Sponsor may substitute prize of equ[al or] greater retail value, if necessary, at its sole discretion.

7. Additional terms: By participating, entrants agree a) to the official rules and decisions of the judges, which will be final in all resp[ects] and to waive any claim to ambiguity of the official rules and b) to release, discharge, and hold harmless HarperCollins, Parac[hute,] Dualstar, and their affiliates, subsidiaries, and advertising and promotion agencies from and against any and all lia[bilities] or damages associated with acceptance, use, or misuse of any prize received in this sweepstakes.

8. Any dispute arising from this Sweepstakes will be determined according to the laws of the State of New York, without reference [to] conflict of law principles, and the entrants consent to the personal jurisdiction of the State and Federal courts located in New [York] County and agree that such courts have exclusive jurisdiction over all such disputes.

9. To obtain the name of the winners, please send your request and a self-addressed stamped envelope (residents of Vermont [may] omit return postage) to THE NEW ADVENTURES OF MARY-KATE & ASHLEY Camp Survival Kit Sweepstakes Win[ners] c/o HarperEntertainment, Attn: Children's Marketing Department, 10 East 53rd Street, New York, NY 10022 by December 1, 2[003.] Sweepstakes Sponsor: HarperCollins Publishers, Inc.

so little time
BOOK SERIES

Based on the hit television series

mary-kate olsen   ashley olsen

so little time
best friends forever

Life is anything but boring for Chloe and Riley Carlson—especially since they've entered high school. Now they're making new friends, meeting new boys, and learning just what being a teenager is all about. No wonder they have so little time!

Coming soon wherever books are sold!

Don't miss the other books in the so little time book series!

- ❏ How to Train a Boy
- ❏ Instant Boyfriend
- ❏ Too Good to be True
- ❏ Just Between Us
- ❏ Tell Me About It
- ❏ Secret Crush

- ❏ Girl Talk
- ❏ The Love Factor
- ❏ Dating Game
- ❏ A Girl's Guide to Guys
- ❏ Boy Crazy

It's What YOU Read.

Real Books for Real Girls

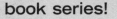

LOG ON!

mary-kateandashley.com
America Online Keyword: mary-kateandashley

DUALSTAR VIDEO

Watch out for the 2004 calendar!

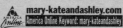

mary-kateandashley.com
America Online Keyword: mary-kateandashley

Ten CDs Performed by Mary-Kate and Ashley

It's
What
YOU
Listen To.

Available where music is sold

Own The Hit Series on *DVD* and Video

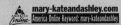

NEW VOLUMES!

It's
What
YOU
Watch.

mary-kateandashley.com
America Online Keyword: mary-kateandashley